Starship Tahiti

Starship Tahiti

Poems

i

Brandon Dean Lamson

UNIVERSITY OF MASSACHUSETTS PRESS

Amherst and Boston

ISBN 978-1-62534-009-2

Designed by Sally Nichols
Set in MrsEaves
Printed and bound by
Thomson-Shore, Inc.

Library of Congress Cataloging-in-Publication Data
Lamson, Brandon Dean.
Starship Tahiti : poems / Brandon Dean Lamson.
pages cm. — (Juniper Prize for Poetry)
Includes bibliographical references.
ISBN 978-1-62534-009-2 (pbk. : alk. paper)
I. Title.
PS3612.A54745S73 2013
811′.6—dc23
2012045697

British Library Cataloguing-in-Publication Data
A catalogue record for this book is available from the British Library.

For as this appalling ocean surrounds the verdant land, so in the soul of man there lies one insular Tahiti, full of peace and joy, but encompassed by all the horrors of the half known life.

— Melville, *Moby Dick* —

For Elizabeth

Contents

III

IV

Acknowledgments

Thanks to the editors and readers of the following journals in which these poems first appeared, sometimes in slightly different versions:

Akkadian: "Crazy Horse & Bondage"
Hunger: "Black Dog, White Dog"
Nano Fiction: "Pit Bull Training"
Pebble Lake Review: "Irises"

"Sonar," "Dark Magus," "Rescue Divers," and "Metallica Burns on the Altar of the Viking Rockstar" first appeared in a chapbook titled *Houston Gothic,* published by LaMunde Press.

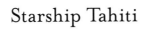

Starship Tahiti

.

Black Dog, White Dog

6am. Grand Central Station. Black dog, white dog,
sprawled beneath a domed ceiling
                                    etched with constellations,
gods and beasts poised
                        to kill or genuflect into the depthless
mirror they're trapped inside.
    Shifting panes creak awake,

a homeless man jarred out of his parka
and star blanket by the clatter of feet.
Suddenly,
            his ceiling has become his floor;
the elevated dais he dreamed he was sleeping on
collapsed
in a construction accident that left a commuter paralyzed.

Black dog, white dog,
leashes tethered to the fist of a blue-eyed deity
taken human form as a grizzled ex-cop
who laces his coffee with Kahlua.
                            Bomb sniffers, paranoiac,
hair trigger snouts.
                    Wet fish eye lenses zooming in
on suspicious fibers,
cosmetic powders made from crushed scarabs.

White dog's hair stands on end,
                        muscles tensed,

while black dog jumps up on the cop's arthritic knee.
He tore the anterior cruciate ligament
on his last SWAT team run,

                    his job always as point man,

shoving the mechanical battering ram

against the door and blowing its hinges,
rushing gun drawn
                 into a cave
full of blaring stereos,
human voices real or synthesized,
                       weed smoke,
angel dust or steam, sounds of expulsion
toilets flushing,
windows shattering and slamming closet doors

as felons reach for shotguns
legal documents or ecstasy stashes,
   women stalling and crying

while their men reach
               into locked boxes
of unbeing and spill their contents
into porcelain mouths.

Black dog, white dog,
               hopped up on bomber's glue,
chasing that dragon, a coiled knot of rusty nails,
strain forward on their leashes,
pulling their limping handler.

He knows he's dead already.
Dirty martyrs digging black holes.

White dog and black dog unearthing
buried skulls bathed in jet fuel.
He gazes at Orion
                    peering down from the ceiling,
his bow drawn taut.

Will the dogs reach it before it detonates,
a surge of white light
                        rippling through
this vaulted chamber.
Dogs see everything.
Human animosity washes over them

like elevator muzak.

Dogs don't do jihad. Their heaven is finding bombs.

Instead, try this filthy sleeper stirring in his parka,
the fur lined collar stiff with grime.
White dog crouches, his muzzle inches away
from the man's shut eyes, and barks.

Black one joins, tail wagging, sniffing powder
residue on the man's half gloved fingers,
whatever he snorted last night.

Un-strapping his holster, the ex-cop waits
for the guy to reach for a ripcord

under his huge coat and detonate,
spraying chunks

           of homeless flesh and metal shards,
a nova flaring hot right here, swallowing them, howling.

The Q101 Bus to Antigone

We board the Q101 bus quietly, like bruises that swell
under hotel room sheets. In the last seat she touches
photos of Juan that are already burning, images
of a teenager posing in his shiny grey suit,
his prom date in high heels that blister her toes.

These are the selves staring from her palms
while he lingers at the rim of a prison toilet bowl,
eager to vomit ghosts.
Rough tongues of hand held metal detectors
frisk me as I enter HDM, the max security jail.

Inside the classroom Juan is one of twenty inmates
laughing or sleeping or banging on their desks.
I write the word *Antigone* on the board,
chalk dusting my fingers not the same used to outline
a body at the heart of a crime scene,

the map of a corpse many convicts claim
never to have seen, even with the murder weapon
registered to their alias, even as their mothers ride
the Q101 bus to Rikers, starburst decals on their red
fingernails clicking against steel railing in the visitor's room.

Pirate Ships

The first time I walk into one of the jailhouses on Rikers
I have to remind myself to breathe. Not only is the stench
of unwashed bodies and mess hall food suffocating,
but I can't focus what's happening.

Lines of convicts waiting for barbershop, dozens of eyes
sweeping over me, I watch myself try to glance at them casually.
They can see right through you dog, they know you're green as hell.
We're close, our shoulders almost brushing as I walk by

and force myself to look at each of them. The woman
who brought me here says she couldn't make eye contact
with any of her students her first few days on the island.

On the third day a soft-spoken Jamaican student called
her to his desk and said, Miss, don't be scared of we pirates.
She looked into his bloodshot eyes softened by contraband
weed and smiled.

Inmates scrutinize me behind masks of cement
and jagged scars, one of them a crescent running
from below an ear to the corner of a mouth, a smiley it's called,

raised keloid tissue pale on darker skin. I remember as a kid
I'd rub the sienna birthmark on the inside of my left thigh
and hope it would always be there.

Prison Letters

Heat sensors can detect where the prison
censor's warm hands opened these letters
searching for a fault line in the gene code.
Any lifeline to the outside that hasn't been
destroyed. A letter that begins *Ramon,*
your mother is very ill. Please mention
to your parole board. Whatever can be stolen
and claimed by thieves is. Most perishable
may be scent, letters soaked in perfumes
or oils to conjure a wild garden of memory
in the dayroom, a candlelit bathtub
of floating rose petals mingled with flashes
of a rival on his knees crying like a bitch.
Unless you separate them these odors
can cripple you, rip your orange jumpsuit
off your shoulders like the flimsy summer
dress of a woman who asked you to protect
her from your older brothers. These letters
sent into a smoldering pit deeper than regret.
More convincing than fingerprints or mug shots,
they escape underground, hijacking mail trucks
and planes to slip outside prison walls.

Razor Dream Sonnet

I feel his razor before I see it pinched between his thumb
and forefinger writing a hot, sticky message that stretches
from below my left ear to my chin. The shamrock inked
on the back of his hand is a fleck of steaming cud spat out
of a bull's mouth. His brethren grab my arms, jacking me
against the mesh screen window. Gashes multiply, flaying
my Italian dress shirt and then my skin, popping buttons.
A meat jacket. Not so much pain as the humiliation of leakage,
the only plucked bird in a butcher shop display case.
A slashed tapestry on the loom of the gods. Half human,
half divine. I bow before a television mounted
to the wall that blares the Jerry Springer Show.
The scrolling text reads: If you know someone
who secretly wants to sleep with his brother, call us now.

Insomnia Sonnet

Nights alone are worst. I reach three feet into the darkness
above my cramped bed and graze prison bars I pass through
daily, teaching inmates how to spell. Rikers Island a fortress
from the twenties immune to renovation. Pulleys and gears
crank gates shut. The only modern equipment a massive stone
chair that's wheeled between cell blocks. Inmates line up before
this medieval throne and rest their chins on the chair's arm
as they sit on its molded seat. The device x-rays four inches
down the prisoner's throat and six inches up his rectum.
Many are caught boofing — slipping razors into a matchbook
cover and jamming them inside their asses. I fantasize
about sitting in the chair, being invaded and scoured clean
by its rays. But I'm only a Board of Education employee.

Exit Wounds — An Interlude

Gary Gilmore shot in the heart.
The firing squad aims,
                camera flashes blink SOS,
winking seductively at the wall that will catch the bullets.

Gilmore wants to die worst of all,
                      he's begging
for blood atonement, his own blood spilled to redeem him.

The Book of Mormon explicit: Christ's blood is wasted
on murderers.
            They must pay with their own.

In the old Utah a council of elders dragged suspects
out of bed and brought them to
                  freshly dug graves.
Forced to bend over sweet smelling troughs,
their throats cut.
            They bled into the bottom.

Gilmore wore a sleeveless black sweatshirt.
His shoelaces were red, white, and blue.
His last seconds, the slim canal the dead
                must pass through.

Afterwards, the tub where his corpse
will be washed of its terror,
              of razor strap beatings

his father delivered, embedded shards
of light bulbs he slit his wrists with.

He said to his brother, if someone beats you,
do not fight back. The hand that murders
washes itself clean, by water, by fire, by blood

and whatever blossoms from its spillage:
leaf, stem, root, pod.

The shirt returned to Gilmore's family
has five bullet holes, not four.

Of the five rifles trained on his chest,
one of them should have fired a blank.

No chances taken.

To his brother Gilmore looked scared not defiant,
afraid he would see the burning field where he stood,

his blood not enough
to douse the blaze before it reaches the forest
where someone washes
                        his victims' feet and hair.

Rose M. Singer

Sam says the women are harder to teach.
Harder than the male inmates
corralled daily into my room,
raging at reflections
in that mirror-less space,
Bison and Menace throwing
punches in the hallway
as guards hit body alarms
and I bear hug Bison from behind.
Harder than the day a female
counselor spoke to my class,
one of those Beckett says
won't let you refuse a cup of coffee,
and the guys in the front row
reached into their FUBU sweats
and pulled out their cocks,
automatons raging against the inferno.
Even harder than that, Sam insists.
We talk this way to survive.
I call on him to prove it.
One morning he got a call to sub
for a math teacher in Rose M. Singer,
a women's jail whose name suggests
a gentle convalescent for flappers
or former jazz greats.
Brought in handcuffed
and in leg shackles,
they were seated at desks
and given short pencils
without erasers, no means of correction,

just cross outs and do overs.
Sam wrote an algebra equation
on the board: $3X + 1 = 2Y$
and asked them to solve for X.
Two students began arguing
about the solution, no single
letter capable of standing
for the rage at what was missing,
and since neither had enough room
to swing, one reached
into her orange jumpsuit,
pulled a used tampon

from her vagina and slapped
the other woman across
the face with it, with X,
Defiant X, *solve that bitch,*
X lost on the linoleum floor,
sweet jelly roll done gone
and left this world of sin,
the substitute for slave names
and the letter etched over
the eyes of the dead.
X, which multiplied and signed
at the end of letters means love.

Pit Bull Training

Barrett Price hands me the tattered magazine, a scroll mapping out
the kingdom of animal souls, *Why I Love My American Pit Bull*
stamped on the cover. I see him waking that morning in his cell
and rifling through his stash of back issues, searching for this one.
I can borrow it until Monday, our next class.

Inside, ads for breeders: Bam-Bam and Red Chief pups — get one now!
And grainy pictures of pits — hulking, barrel-chested, squat bow legs
and anvil heads filled with rows of shark teeth. Lolling tongues, grimaces
and smiles. In the background, dirt roads and patches of grass, trailer park
tableaus, tin roofs and mesh fences you could stick your fist through.

Barrett's got two champion pits on his uncle's farm in North Carolina:
one brindle and one red, taking turns hanging from a tire swing lashed
to an old oak. Testing their jaw strength, he'd fill a kiddie pool with ice
cold water and drag it under the suspended dogs, waiting for one to drop.

Approaching jail, I see a gull tangled in razor wire, its wings splayed,
larger than I imagined. Mites devour its eyes; planes soar overhead,
destined for LaGuardia. Dogs and men pace inside cages. Ruthless
canines. Breeders match dogs. Girlfriends take their men into corners

of the visiting room and discreetly lift their skirts. Mating fields raked
into scorched grass. Birth given in project hallways, or beneath concrete
blocks that raise trailers off the ground. How much space inside your skull
do you need to breathe?

II

Storming the Warehouse

Praise be the river finders
and their currents of healing estuary.

The yellow boombox throbbing
on the motel dresser as she straddles me,

her face pierced by fish hooks and beads
the color of salmon eggs.

I drive her back to the park where swaths
of green bisect the city into encampments

of corporate flow. Her Indian friend Mighty Mouse
recruits me for the tribal basketball team,

We ain't so tall, but we got moves.
Follow the river. Purchase a board and cruise

to the skate park near the Columbia Bridge underpass.
She swore I'd find them here, homeless kids

they call trolls soliciting tribute, goat shepherdesses
selling broken staffs as Cerebus sprawls beside them,

a duffel bag of greased barrels without triggers.
Afternoon stunt tricks and withdrawal,

the king's men racing above from castle to castle,
office high rise to luxury condo.

I am not speaking of the bridge,
rather of plywood ramps and lean-tos

on these river banks the Indians shunned,
calling Portland the valley of sickness.

Praise be the river finders, river of suffering,
no Ganges of burning pyres, this Columbia

where suicides are peppered with cloud spray.
She rides me in the motel room as Fugazi

pummels her boombox, her face the face
of my cousin in pain except he's 6'8" and bearded.

Let our feet trail bandages as we storm
the Doc Martens warehouse, ransacking aisles

for boots, ox-blood and steel-toed, plastered
with pink skulls or green shamrocks that glow

in the dark as we march to the castle gates,
our torches hissing in the rain.

Evidence
after Luc Sante

Shot in the room, a faint popping sound
of glass sprayed his lap like rain.

No, he was killed outside, backed into an alley,
maybe begging on his knees, looking up
at swaying laundry lines,

                       the white sheets out of reach.
Then dragged to a back room for someone to find.

I can't tell from the photo, circa 1914;
could he see danger darken the edges of the room
sepia toned,

                or was everything sudden as seizure?

Death is not a child on a parade route, is not
held aloft to catch prizes thrown to the crowd.

Who knows when the child will ask to climb
down into your arms?
You both see the sky's changes,

                       thunderstorms
mingling with sunlight, weather a friend of mine
calls "the devil beats his wife."

Sometimes the dying show themselves:
in a transvestite bar

I met a man without legs
who propelled himself across the floor on a skateboard
and asked me to lift him onto a barstool.

Placing my hands on either side of his ribcage,
I lifted him from the grip tape
                              and thought how rough
the tape must feel
                  against his stumps, his ghost limbs
singing crickets in a burning field.

After drinking several hours
he told me having no legs
                          was like always sitting,
moving from station to station on a train that never stops,
a conductor who never says let's see your ticket
or stand up and move along now.

Anything can disappear; a flier taped to the wall
announces a woman missing since Christmas,
                          her Xeroxed photo
outlined in thick black,
                          crude, indefinite, embarrassing
because it is the one photo of ourselves
we'll never see, tossed into a metal drawer
and lost like all the sirens I've missed or the beatings
I've closed my eyes through.

Buddha's Robes

The Diamond Sutra begins,

After begging for food in the city

and eating his meal of rice,
the Bhagavan put his robe and bowl away, washed his feet,
and sat down.

During his morning rounds sparrows dove from dusty trees
and stole grains of rice from the bowl he held steady for them,

so the seamstress who ladled the rice into his bowl
was feeding the birds who woke her at sunrise, singing
on a branch outside her window.

Be without a self, without

a being, without a life, without a soul.
Wearing his patched robe

frayed like a cloak of leaves, burnt oranges and yellows
mended and worn until their colors blend.

In Baltimore, men gather on street corners at dusk
sharing tins of food with mongrels
they've saved from sodium pentothal and dogfights.

Years later in D.C. I worked in a furniture store
assembling wrought iron chairs and huge marble tables,
their surfaces shot through

with veins of green and black,
like a meteorologist's chart predicting ceaseless downpour.

During lunch I walked to the stoop on the corner
                              where Floyd and his crew hung out,
Floyd smiling as he did the first day
he asked me for change then offered me a drink.

The seams in his face cracked open,

                    a Yoruban mask studded with nails
to let the spirits out,
red bandanna tied around his dreads now darkened to rust.

I sat with them as we passed around a forty bottle
and drank cold malt liquor,
                              observing suits gliding by
several feet in front of their coffins.

White Power

And blessed is the lion
that becomes man when consumed by man,
and cursed is the man whom the lion consumes,
and the lion becomes man.

In lion garb I drive among the oblivious,
the Janus-faced Jesus freak pranksters
and salesman broadcasting from churches large as hangars.

They shalt not consume me.

Outside Autozone a man asks for change,
saying he's just been released from county.
I give him two bucks and he lifts his stained t-shirt
showing off a tattooed cross between his shoulders
drawn with a child's deliberate hand,
and below, inked letters spelling WHITE.

How does he know, my zippers
and seams hidden, I've paced
cages where raw meat is seasoned
to taste, tenderized with mallets, wrapped
in plastic and shipped to various destinations
where jobs and shelter are denied?

Does he believe I'm a man as he is —
white duplicates itself in vicious glimmers

or that if I destroy him I will become him,
bending him over the hood of my wagon
in a pearl-handled embrace that cuts heavenly,
vapor steaming celestial glass, a cleaning?

Finding Lola Savannah

I wake every morning at four, her warmth no longer there,
the bare shoulder with its heart and thorns.

Regular practice of inversion increases blood flow to the brain,
while backbends elongate the spine and open the heart chakra.

Sunblind, one may enter a shaded canopy and imitate poses
of animals that emerge at night to feed.

I wander onto a porn shoot in a Houston warehouse
and she's groaning on the mattress, her burgundy nails
clawing another man's freckled back.

Yogis have been known to hold their breath underwater for nearly
twenty minutes.

If you paint temporary tattoos on an actor's throat, then film her
being strangled, the same telescoping effect would occur.

On break I wander next door to Lola Savannah
where exotic coffee beans are roasted,
burlap sacks stamped with names of their sultry origins:

Ghana and Jamaica piled onto Sumatra and Costa Rica.

In a small room near the back a bearded man wears goggles
and turns the roaster, green hulls inside growing darker as
the scent of their essential oils is released.

Knights of Fidelity

After nightfall a black telescopic ray prodded my mind
and I tore apart my den searching for the emergency
contact sheet filled with highlighted numbers.

One of them would answer, Ray or Delroy or Angus,
lucid and radiant with ease like headlights sweeping
over a wet roof, bathing each storm tossed branch,

not blaming the damage they may have caused.
Why ditch the last meeting on consolidated risk factors
that may lead to cancerous urges toward obsessively measuring

your own body parts? I joined the Knights of Fidelity to quell
the tapping of lemurs in my closet, their sticky finger pads
wrapped around gleaming bars and hangers, anchors

for a spillage of couture never worn. Tropical silks shat
by wide eyed monkeys. Angus says call Arien, the girl
in our support group whose invitation read: *Come*

to my apartment for a nude beach party.
I enjoy stripping and showing off as much as any successful
Fidelity graduate, having worked the program to cleanse

myself of blockages and inhibitions that dampen energy flow.
I may even, through well-documented powers of self-deception,
be able to pretend a one bedroom hovel in Queens is swept

by rolling surf. The word *party* is the equivocator.
All those eyes luring me into the center of a mirage
or courtyard or pool with ocean view, except I'll be

the only one naked, tricked by my fellow knights
into this premeditated exposure captured by a ubiquitous
cam recorder for repetitive viewing at my next self esteem

support group. The bachelor stripped bare descending
a warped staircase that plunges into the darkness of Madagascar,
ring-tailed lemurs hurling feces and a shotgun on the closet floor.

Mud Man Plays the Copenhagen Jazz Fest

We wander into Vandkunsten Square as sheets
of saxophone unfurl over cobblestone,
musicians honking onstage.
Another such space we just came from,
a church we found, massive organ pipes
flanking an altar, curved beams jealous
of their breathy cousins down the street.
We'd survived your sister's Danish wedding,
toast after toast droning Nordic pathos
like live fish tossed at the market,
slippery and numb on delicate beds of herbs
and spicy marinades. So when,
because my sister-in-law is Mexican,
the mariachis arrive, their tight black
suits the skin of ripened fruit,
half the party rises to dance,
to pound out fever, sparks shooting
from eyes and mouths. Eventually
the Danes begin shifting side to side,
their zipped up costumes taken out
of a meat locker to thaw.
The next day you and I travel
to Christiania, the fabled commune
in the center of Copenhagen.
I imagined translated versions of the Haight,
tribes draped in love beads and peasant
dresses that skirted their dirty feet.
We enter the gates, past booths of tourist
wares and into squares of makeshift
bars raised on stilts. Then darkness:
surrounded by gutter punks swathed

in spiked leathers, dreads haloed by weed
smoke and below, scarred faces familiar
with knives and knuckles. I pull you closer
as the prison inside me breaks through
and I'm there again, in the yard before a riot,
blacks playing drums as Dominicans reach
into their pants. All my tentacles extend:
I don't need anyone to speak my language.
As we step through a hole punched
in a corrugated tin wall, we see a man
walking toward us naked from the waist up,
completely covered in mud.
A mud man who nods as he passes,
his eyes poking through the mask.

Portland Bardo

The fragile, in between state of larvae hatching
      is no less desirable than full bloom in a city of roses,
if such a city can ever be found.
      I drove toward it once, through forests smoked with fog,
toward what Indians once called the valley of sickness,

a place where animals staggered off to die.
      Always I sought the below ground,
and when I arrived I slept in the basement
      of a youth hostel where foreign tongues spoke softly
like the murmur of stalactites dripping into cups of veined rock.

Read stories of miners trapped in a partial collapse,
      rescuers' attempts to pipe oxygen into the shale tombs
and their reluctance to dig for fear of disturbing
      a labyrinth of tenuous shafts. As I lay there
numerous insertions were threaded through my body,

so when three days later J brought an ambrosia
      tipped needle to my fur, I dilated for the stinger.
But bees don't pollinate roses, they damage
      silky petals infused with blood, unable to absorb
any further sweetness. This isn't a story to be rushed.

Homeless I wandered the parks stepping lightly
      as though on a path of crushed oyster shells,
their insides shucked and hissing.
      It rained and rained and rained.
The scorched disaster I'd driven to escape

still burned my mind, its rafters draped
       with geese and something larger
split down the middle and hung by its ankles.
       Where I grew up, when a house was struck
by lightning we'd drive by and look,

its blackened frame changed
       into what would never again be refuge,
so complete was its new expression,
       yet no one would demolish it. I'm sure
the earth tried hard to deliver it

as dawn light made the searing more real,
       like those bodies found hanging from trees
inside the gates of Chinatown as punishment
       warning those who would betray the Fa-gong,
attempt to escape the maze of tunnels that run

beneath the grand facades of restaurants,
       steaming platters of fish and birds' nests
served through swinging kitchen doors and below,
       in the catacombs, a shipment
of black tar heroin taped to a courier's hairless chest.

So the city's strata are revealed petal by thorn
       as exotic imports of scavenged twigs,
glittering scales and crushed poppies.
       If I could have lain in a field of them,
a crimson entourage dusting my lips and eyelids,

and the girl's, and the lion's, we three the first to fall,
        but instead I woke in a Motel 6 bathroom
with a girl's painted toes in my mouth,
        the lion snarling on the nosecone of a fighter plane
that spun through blue and white clouds blazing to gold.

Carried beyond bombed schoolhouses
        where I'd first suffered, playgrounds strewn
with blazers and slacks I'd grown out of
        year after year, memorizing the same song:
between the river and the bay there is a school we love,

it guides us on and lights the way sure as the stars above.
        When I woke again,
only the city remained outside the cab of my black truck.
        The girl vanished;
she'd skinned the lion and wore his coat as a thong.

Hooked, what does that mean?
        Fleeced, more like it. Or unmasked,
the wizard's holographic image flickering
        as it dies and the curtain is ripped away
revealing a beast with wings.

III

Rescue Divers

Waking in a second story room on St. Charles Street, sheet pulled back
around a strange woman's waist, dragon tattoo flaring across her breast

like a medieval brand hissing after a night of hot strikes and cooling salve.
Naked, I glimpse through the curtain to the balcony, wrought iron

railing that trellises morning light, smells of chicory and magnolias.
Two nights ago an Israeli woman taught my brother and me how

to assemble an AK 47, drawing diagrams on a napkin wet with Hurricanes.
I wake beside my brother in our hotel room, both of us scared

to cross the hall and knock on father's door, suspecting he's been
swept away on a makeshift raft of silicone breasts and liquor crates.

We wander through Magnolia Projects to buy shrimp po-boys
at King's Deli, Otis Redding's "These Arms of Mine" wafting through

a tattered screen door. Being visited and rescued and sung to for no reason.
Last night I left with the Queen of Dragons and her Mohawk friend

leaned close, saying he'd kill me if I hurt her. Handed a leaflet
on Bourbon Street declaiming hellfire and the wages of sin,

I find grammatical mistakes and assess its flammability.
Fucking without protection, deltas flooded brackish and heaving,

water wings, unaware thousands will drown here, attended
by a morning light that empties me into increasingly clear vessels,

smoky glass turning amber. I'm face down on the sheets.
Hester wraps my hair around her fist and pulls

and I wake on my knees beside the river slowly
undulating around the city as it prepares to submerge.

Starship Tahiti

I see Gauguin feverish and dreaming.

There is no cure unless casually accepting
death is one,
        the way Tahitian girls kneel
on the straw mat beside his bed.

I like to think angels falter,
occasionally turn their divine gaze
on satyrs who are tangling hooves below,
savoring the months of heaviness.

We want to mix immunity with the divine,
forgetting gods took the shape of animals to seduce us.

In Chinese opera everyone dies:
the man, the woman, and the other man
neutered down to a few gestures.

Before you finish undressing
let me change the light bulb,
               blue is better,
now this is our Antarctica,
our perpetual half-light in which nothing ends.

Clavicles steeped in blue shadow,
            above us stars
glow on my tapestry,
and if you look past either pole of us,
mouth or ass, there is a rip
in the ozone, a glimpse of afterlife.

The Prophecy of Miss Branch

She said many things that were false and I never claimed
she was beautiful except when her face was reflected in the pond.

But her voice constantly woke me to things
I thought were taboo, the pleasure of being hurt, of hurting back.

The first night with her I remember hearing my neighbor's
short wave radio, wondering if the high pitched noises

were spirits falling into something bigger than themselves,
and the next morning she wore a low cut blouse

to show off the bruises I gave her. She said locusts
were the cursed angels God banishes to be crushed beneath

our feet. I found evil like that parasitic, grotesque.
I asked her, why scars, why do I have scars and she said

so God can recognize you by your suffering, though I knew
sometimes it comes so fast He can't possibly see. She

made me feel things other than fear as though plague
were a boy I could lure into my car with sticky sweets,

smother him in the backseat. We'd bury him with pictures
of our friends so if he woke up he'd kill them first.

Crazy Horse & Bondage

The whip looped around the back of the chair
he's on his stomach anticipating the spark,
gun-powder packed between vertebrae
she's clapping like they're at a birthday party
the handle of the whip smooth as the pony's neck
she never got *Potlach* the Indian word for exchange
Crazy Horse's grandmothers cut skin off their forearms
for his sacred bundle in return he fasted & prayed
crouched in a pit on the third day he saw spirit horses
diving toward him & white riders who shook rain
from their hair she pulls his chin back, wraps the whip
around his throat he hasn't been this scared since
acting class where he was told to remember almost
drowning unlike Crazy Horse he is no prophet
she speaks calmly enough to start a riot he doesn't
pray no one prays for him relax she says & raises
welts stereo speakers blast death metal more lights
strange voices & it would be an interrogation
giving in is seductive telling her where the money
is hid she's a material girl diamonds pearls
she's the duchess seated across in the stagecoach
who lifted her skirt & slapped him when he looked
he's the double agent who's in a jam next stop
firebombed Dresden cracking the whip she resembles
his father snapping his belt to show how it would hurt
Crazy Horse knew the white man's stinger the repeating rifle
Crazy Horse was the last chief to enter the fort
soldiers bound his wrists & paid another Oglala
to stab him in the back lashed onto a rubber sheet
he closes his eyes as she pisses a warm flow on his chest
Crazy Horse was never photographed & in that sense

never captured her fingers gently massage his scars
only one of them speaks English he pays her $300
every other week whipping him is like unbraiding
his hair loosening the strands of his story

Dark Magus

I'm listening to Miles Davis wail abstract versions
of Sly Stone's funk. Black Asiatic voodoo,
Bengal tigers suspended by ropes of braided hemp,
skinned by delicate boned men in green silk shirts.
Eye of the vulture scanning a marbled red topography
beneath the tiger's flayed skin; rivered veins,
arterial tributaries flowing through the earth's core,
a cooling heart. To the west, California spins
its mystic juju, silicon despair, cement impressions
of celebrity hands & feet, my woman's combat boots
tossed beside the mattress. Her grip squeezing
my shoulders here & here. To the east, New York City
charges admission to its warped carnival,
a rainbow shooting gallery. Bodies cheating bodies.
Diamond-studded ears. Showtime at the Apollo.
Santeria in Brooklyn. Roosters crowing Go away,
go now, let the straight razor's melody slash your throat,
let it push you out adorned & ruthlessly pursuing
an escape from this lavish maze of jungle noise & panic,
of thumping bass lines like kisses reviving
that sleeping black prince.

Cannibal Headdress

We wake up fused, unwashed sweat and dread knots
    our cannibal headdress. We couple like beasts,
skull beads braided in our hair.
    Untangling us will be mystical like removing bandages
from skin grafting this world to the underworld.

Her three year old son Malachi screams
    in the next room, trashing the make believe
garage where cars are idling, ready to take him away.
    For half an hour he rages, smashing his toys,
kicking the door and howling when words fail.

After his mother has left and I'm walking
    at night along yellow lines of a road that winds
through the mountains, hoping to be struck,
    I hear wolves and pine trees creaking,
each needle searching my body for warmth.

Irises

Morning in the blue room, nothing disguised, night
dragged under the bed. Our antics a portable stage

which withdrew come daylight. The arch of my foot
grazed your calf, urging it toward the windowsill,

irises blooming, climbing vines trellising the wall
fallen into ruin. Caress every fourth blossom,

gently cut the stem, then bring them through the window.
We can afford to let that much in.

Billie Holiday Sings at the Starlight

Intermission was like when we slept, our backs touching.

The blue lights at the end of the film reel
were never kind to us; when they came on
across the street we should have stopped,

gone over to the Starlight Inn
and ordered drinks, sang Billie Holiday tunes
until the universe expanded, then shrank
to the density of a white dwarf,
a spotlight keen on stage.

There will never be enough sheets, enough darkness.
Your hands covered your eyes and I wondered what you saw.

IV

Filming the Explosion

It may arrive as a silence,
                              a clearing stumbled upon in a forest
when all you searched for was the old graveyard.

Possibly in those same woods, late November,
when gunshots whizzed
                              close enough to make your ears sting
with the shattered horns of a twelve point buck.

Maybe it waited for you in a tree stand,
beneath a sky pearling at sunset & streaked
like a shell whose creature has died,

as you did on mornings when another drinking spell ended
& shame handwrote your deeds & shoved its list
into a bottle of Grey Goose.

How long can you live inside yourself unharmed?

All the men in the forest are you;
when they're well behaved you celebrate
by taking them out to the stadium for a ball game,
all of them chained together & shouting for different teams.

Years later you read about South African police
testing booby trapped headphones
by fastening them around the heads of decapitated pigs
& filming the explosions.

There are no assassins here.
The headphones lie on the table in front of you.

You remember stopping at Bobby's Liquor Store
on your way to school, your father telling the black men
loitering outside *ten dollars on two*
& inside the store he bought you grape Nehi & Ho-Hos

for breakfast, setting them on the counter
next to jars of jellied pig's feet & knuckles.
Pig's feet, dear God.

Tropicana Drag

I fall into that orange van, circa 1976. My parents
let me choose from a book of color samples: ten varieties
of blue and how many names do we have for sorrow?
I stretch out on the floor of our van painted tangerine,
windows tinted black, and spy on the world.
My head a six year old satellite dish.
Mother said I could even get undressed
and no one would see me though I'm not sure I believe
her after the accident in last year's car, rear ended
at a stoplight, glass dusting my shoulders, pulverized wings,
and I was afraid someone was kneeling on the trunk,
chipping through the back window with an ice pick.
The place where I am safe is orange. A screened porch,
Fourth of July; Black Cat fireworks explode, showering
the river's blue party mask, us kids allowed to run
with sparklers, inventing new constellations traced
in orange around our waists. Mother's flashy scarf
in her lap. She drinks Tom Collins endlessly.
Sometimes honey, I'm not myself. The little kids
taunt the dog making him jackknife in mid air.
I'm too big to play their games. Orange is the aura
of removal, my parent's bedroom door. The color
hunters wear. And convicts when they clean the road.
Felony is the name of an orange bird and a beautiful name
for a girl. She'd be my age and we'd play Saturday
Night Fever, dance and sing falsetto. Maybe I chose
the sound orange made in my mouth. Tubes of orange
lipstick growing in vines. Lush masquerade, a new alias:
Miss Roseanna Tropicana. Still the picture describes itself.
If I remember she wore lilac and we practically carried
her to the van.

Sonar

Bats are trapped in my grandparent's cabin, screeching,
their wings battering the air ducts. We unscrew
the metal plates over the ventilation shaft and hold
a plastic garbage bag over the opening

so when they hurtle toward the rift in the wall they fly
not into the bedroom papered with peeling roses
but into a net cinched over them. Enraged,
their lunar clicks return holographic waves of seamless black.

Mother balances on a desk chair as the bats rush
into the bag that billows over her shoulder. She intends
to carry them into the back yard where plastic owls hang
from the branches of the cherry tree. My brother

and I are shouting, running in and out of the room,
leathery wings of bats soft like feathers encased in a pillow sack.
Inside out — shouldn't the feathers be closest to our skin,
settling in our ears as we sleep and the wings rip through?

Father waits on the lawn, gripping his Louisville Slugger.
They've already told us about the night they woke to a bat
whirling above their canopy bed, how he took his army jacket
from the closet and caught it in the dark green folds.

And squeezed. That night I caught him smothering her
I froze in the doorway. She's closed the bag, nearly falling

from the chair as we scatter down porch stairs and she follows,
hissing *you babies,* the plastic bag releasing dismembered scraps

that need to be moved. She calls father by his name
where he stands ready to strike, *No Larry,* and flings the bag
onto the ground, stepping back as the winged fists rise and spread,
suddenly enormous and frayed like kites flown through a burning attic.

Psalm of Sambo

Saplings hacked down with a machete,
flexible switches bending

                  like car antennae above
a hood stenciled with flames.

A black lab named Sambo roaming
Starkey's farm,

          swept under the wheels of the judge's truck.

They buy another black lab and call it Sambo,
then another,

          a pack of Sambos trampled
by the drunken headlights of justice.

Dig a pit in the clearing, lash the saplings
together in the shape

              of a dome and cover it
with hides still wet from skinning.

Crawl inside the membrane abuzz with angel flies.
Consider what you've destroyed,

                the cypress endangered,
slashed from bearded roots to make your lodge of prayer.

Strike a flint and behold the marbled underlayer
of our skin, hit and run,

             Sambo ripped open

dreaming of the next Sambo,

                                runaway Sambo,

our Sambo of solar eclipse

casting earth into the blackness of pearl.

Church Burning in Southern Maryland

I'm back at Trinity Church, Reverend Collins preaching
the gospel of the serpent come down to earth
walking and talking like a man. Those who live
by the sword shall die by the sword he shouts,
urging us to rise as the choir sings
that old rugged cross, twelve women
swaying as one, and my father says
you should have heard them ten years ago
when they were younger. When white fires
spread we lose space to cry in, organ pipes
melting into pools; we forget how deep
our scars, how enduring. Not ten years
or ten thousand. Century old starlight
shines on the flaring match. Stop there Judas,
do not incinerate the robes we will wear
come Sunday. The deacons' hearts gallop
away toward the Chesapeake; you can hear
our thirst for water, another body to climb inside
of holy, holy, gathering on the scorched patch of grass
where their church burned with captive anger
not yet extinguished, those floorboards scuffed
by our best shoes now wood that sobs
smoke and ash of our rhythms, ash of our prayer.

Strange Fruit on Bourbon Street

Dexter Gordon wipes his face with a paisley handkerchief
before "Don't Explain." Sinuous grooves, smoke rising
from mouths, cables to heaven. Sometimes beauty

is too much & the changing structure of the song
overwhelms us, opening riffs of loss
that will never end but repeat, a refrain of the mind's slur.

Dexter's "Strange Fruit": black men hanging from magnolias,
an afternoon in New Orleans. Balcony chatter before dinner,
slanted light on flesh toned walls.

I started listening to jazz during the era of wet dreams,
"Nights in Tunisia," the pleasure of rewinding the tape.
Which we never can. Father took me to see "Tightrope"

starring Clint Eastwood as an undercover cop.
I was scared, kept seeing men in theater darkness
undressed to what I wanted, taste of rock salt & Georgian clay.

Father would kill me. Clint drinks & gambles off duty,
now he slips a garrote around a Cajun's neck & pulls
tight, embracing him from behind in a stiff dance.

Operate among shadows he seems to say, this city is permissive,
learn from it. There is shouting on Bourbon Street,
but I can't tell whether it's a riot or a party.

Metallica Burns on the Altar of the Viking Rockstar

It was thrash in a steel town. Day jobs as night managers
tending an oracle

                of gasoline fires and industrial accidents.
Flaming suddenly into verse and chorus
they wanted to be poured into glass bottles and hurled.

This was their first album. Before detox.
Before therapy, forced to cut their hair and reflect.

The awkward postures of youth resemble
something molting,

               ripping through
a hairy pod and spitting goo
from its mandibles, waving its praying mantis limbs
in a strobe lit cloud of pheromones.

The first recording I ever made
was in the basement of my grandmother's house —

my friend Charlie and I told stories

                      into a tape player
describing the exploits of Vikings who pillaged
and fucked their way through southern Maryland.

I'd read many fantasy novels,
but I liked the cover illustrations
best, paintings of muscled heroes armed

with swords
        and women clothed in animal skins
kneeling or chained or thrown
over the hero's shoulder.

My friend, a foster kid, showed me the scars
on his stomach and legs from numerous skin grafts.

When he was an infant
        his mother dropped him
in boiling water or spilled it on him, accidentally
or not and he was taken
from her and raised by our neighbor,
a drunken army lieutenant.

I imagine him compelled to speak by an indescribable pain
inflicted on him before he knew words.

Our stories overlapped and entangled
as we recorded them,
        stopped and replayed the tape
to hear our voices.

Thrill of an exotic beast captured,
prowling the yard, the pattern
        of its striped coat shifting
as its muscles lengthened.

                    Once the tape was found
my punishment was to listen
while my parents and grandparents blasted it
at the dining room table.

Dear elders, I'm still shaming you,
writing it down now so you can't erase the pulverizing drum.

Go ahead, you can taste
this paper lubricated with semen and bourbon;
it's flammable,
and your names may be written there, leaves
destined for a manual
on how to become a Viking Rockstar.

'Bama Barbershop

After the latest tragedy grief seeks a voice
beyond the fields and the barn's rough weathering
so I drove faster, tuned into the " 'Bama Hour"
on the A.M. My windows rolled down,
I could smell tobacco drying; beyond
open barn doors, sheaves hung in darkness.
Jerry Washington, aka the 'Bama,
played five versions of "Stormy Monday" back to back
as though he knew what I wanted. Howlin' Wolf sang
The eagle flies on Friday. On Saturday dogs begin to howl.
I wandered through the soul's barrios.
Between songs the 'Bama said she's never coming back.
Parker's Creek Road is a dead end; I drove down
it just for fun. I remember as a boy pressing my face
against the window of a black barbershop.
People inside waved to me like I was a lamb.
Their hands were paintbrushes.
We'd never appear in any murals.
Pee Wee, the barber, said naw, I don't cut white hair.
I wanted to sit in the chair, have him spin me until
I was a blur in the mirror.
'Bama, you really took me for a whirl.
Sadness and I shared the porch swing.
Then I never thought about cutting my hair,
fire under my pillow, overflowing the sink.
Pee Wee said what will Judge Lamson think
if I mess up your head? I sat on boxes of corn liquor
behind the chairs and watched him work.
He raised the customer's chin the way some women
have pulled my face toward theirs then fled,
leaving enough gas money on the bed stand

to get from here to the delta. Ask me why
the 'Bama's passing away into light which hovers
over the fields, that sound of a bottleneck guitar
makes me feel I can never afford another heart break,
another trial separation. Mondays are for funerals.
We can die on the weekend, and even the black Christ
must someday rise.

Notes

"Exit Wounds – An Interlude." This poem draws on material from Mikal Gilmore's memoir about his brother's execution titled *Shot in the Heart*.

"Rose M. Singer." The poem's title is drawn from the Rose M. Singer Center, a women's prison on Riker's Island.

"Evidence." The poem's title is borrowed from Luc Sante's book *Evidence*, which contains 55 crime scene photos from New York City police archives.

"Buddha's Robes." The poem excerpts lines from Red Pine's translation of *The Diamond Sutra*.

"White Power." The poem contains lines from *The Gospel of Thomas*.

"Finding Lola Savannah." The poem contains a reference to Lola Savannah, a coffee company in Houston, Texas.

"Crazy Horse & Bondage." The poem owes a debt to Peter Matthiessen's book *In the Spirit of Crazy Horse*.

"Psalm of Sambo." *The Story of Little Black Sambo* was a children's book written and illustrated by Helen Bannerman, and was first published in 1899. In 1932, Langston Hughes called it a typical "pickaninny" storybook that was hurtful to black children.

"Strange Fruit on Bourbon Street." The poem draws certain details from the 1984 film *Tightrope* starring Clint Eastwood.

"Metallica Burns on the Altar of the Viking Rockstar." This poem was inspired in part by the 2004 Metallica documentary *Some Kind of Monster.*

" 'Bama Barbershop." The poem references Jerry Washington's blues radio show "The 'Bama Hour," which aired on WPFW, a local radio station in Washington, D.C.

The
Juniper
Prize

This volume is the 37th recipient of the
Juniper Prize for Poetry presented annually by the
University of Massachusetts Press for a volume of
original poetry. The prize is named in honor of
Robert Francis (1901–1987), who lived for many years
at Fort Juniper, Amherst, Massachusetts.